Sparkleton
The Haunted Woods

READ MORE SPARKLETON BOOKS!

1

Sparkleton
The Magic Day
BY CALLIOPE GLASS
HARPER Chapters

2

Sparkleton
The Glitter Parade
BY CALLIOPE GLASS
HARPER Chapters

3

Sparkleton
The Mini Mistake
BY CALLIOPE GLASS
HARPER Chapters

4

Sparkleton
The Weirdest Wish
BY CALLIOPE GLASS
HARPER Chapters

5

Sparkleton
The Haunted Woods
BY CALLIOPE GLASS
HARPER Chapters

HARPER **Chapters**

Sparkleton
The Haunted Woods

BY CALLIOPE GLASS

ILLUSTRATED BY
HOLLIE MENGERT

HARPER

An Imprint of HarperCollins Publishers

To Free,

the spookiest horse I ever loved.

Sparkleton #5: The Haunted Woods
Library of Congress Control Number: 2021934343
ISBN 978-0-06-300456-6 — ISBN 978-0-06-300455-9 (paperback)
The artist used Photoshop to create the digital illustrations for this book.
Typography by Andrea Vandergrift
21 22 23 24 25   EP   10 9 8 7 6 5 4 3 2 1

First Edition

TABLE OF CONTENTS

1

It's an Emergency!

Sparkleton galloped all the way to Gramma Una's classroom.

"I've got a glitterrific new plan!" the shaggy unicorn yelled as he burst into the glen. He had stayed up all night working on his plan. It had blueprints. It had checklists. And it was going to work. He just knew it.

"I'm finally going to get wish-granting magic!" Sparkleton told everyone.

But his classmates were too busy talking to each other to pay any attention to him.

SPARKLETON
Hates studying, period

WILLOW
Only likes to study goblin lore

I studied for this test all night!

I made a hundred flash cards!

BRITTA
Pretends to love to study

ROSIE
Loves to study

Oh mud. Sparkleton had forgotten all about the big wilderness survival test! He shuffled his hooves nervously.

"I know *everything* about woodscraft now," Zuzu said.

"Oh yeah?" Britta asked her. "Pop quiz! What's the Unicorn Star?"

"It's the star that never moves in the sky!" Zuzu answered with confidence. "It's super bright. It's always in the same spot. And you can use it to find your way at night!"

"Easy," Britta said.

Sparkleton winced. He'd never even *heard* of the Unicorn Star.

What's the big deal with the Unicorn Star, anyway? Sparkleton wondered. He had found a way to get wish-granting magic! That was so much more exciting! A bunch of Sparkleton's friends had already gotten their magic. Dale had his super-speed magic! Gabe had confetti magic! And Twinkle, the most annoying foal in Shimmer Lake, had gotten *wish-granting* magic! Sparkleton was tired of waiting—and tired of studying!

"Hey, guys, I've got a shimmerrific new plan!" Sparkleton tried again. But they still weren't listening.

"I hope I pass the test," Willow was saying to Gabe. "I really, *really* want to go on the class camping trip. Maybe I can spot a goblin in the woods!"

Sparkleton froze. "Wait . . ." he said. "If you don't pass the test, you can't go on the camping trip?"

His friend Gabe frowned. "Yeah, Gramma Una explained that about seven hundred times last week," he said. "Weren't you listening?"

Sparkleton had *not* been listening. He'd been thinking about his plan.

I have to figure out a way to stop this test from happening, Sparkleton thought.

"Twinkle!" he cried.

Sparkleton trotted over to his classmate.

"I need you to grant a wish for me! It's an emergency!"

It *was* an emergency, after all. Just not for anybody else.

Twinkle's eyes went wide. "An emergency?!" she said. "Oh no! Quick, how can I help?"

"I wish . . . fortenskunks!" Sparkleton said very fast. He was pretty sure you could still grant a wish even if you didn't understand it.

"Ten whats?" Twinkle said. "Ten stumps?"

"Don't worry about it," Sparkleton said. "Just grant the wish. It's an emergency, remember?"

Twinkle nodded.

"Okay," she said. "Just focus really hard on ten stumps or whatever it is."

She quickly stamped her front hooves: *one, two.* Then she lowered her nose and traced a figure eight in the air with her horn. Finally, she looked straight into Sparkleton's eyes.

"Thy wish is granted," she said.

Sparkleton held his breath and thought about ten skunks.

For a moment, everything was perfectly quiet. Perfectly still.

Had his wish worked?

Oh mud! Sparkleton already made a WISH? This can't be good!

2

Utter Mayhem! Pandemonium! Skunks Everywhere!

There was a loud *POP* and a flash of light.

And suddenly, there were skunks *everywhere*.

"Eeek!" Britta whinnied. One of the skunks had landed on her head!

The skunk looked as scared as Britta. It raised its tail and sprayed her right in the face. Then it scampered off into the woods in a panic.

"*Gah!*" Britta cried, scraping at her face with her front legs. "Blargh!"

Sparkleton's eyes watered. The smell was really horrible.

"Skunks!" Rosie yelled. "Everywhere!"

"Run!" Zuzu shrieked.

Suddenly everyone was moving—fast. Sparkleton watched, eyes wide. Gabe tripped over Rosie and went tumbling. Zuzu leapt over Dale, who was zooming out of the clearing as fast as he could go. Dale crashed into Gabe and then *Dale* went tumbling! And every single book in the classroom glen got knocked over.

And then, just like that, it was over.

The skunks had all run in one direction. The young unicorns had all run in the other. Sparkleton was standing in the wreckage all by himself. The classroom glen was quiet.

And it smelled *awful*.

The test would definitely have to be rescheduled.

Mission accomplished! Sparkleton thought. He trotted out to the meadow to find his friends.

"Wasn't that sparkletastic?" Sparkleton said. "My plan to cancel the test worked! Now we don't have to worry about it!"

"You did that on *purpose*?" Britta said angrily. She still smelled pretty bad. Sparkleton wrinkled his nose. "We spent all night studying!"

"Sorry," he told her. "But there was no way I could take the test today!"

"Whatever," Britta said angrily. "I am *so*

mad." She marched away. Zuzu, Dale, Twinkle, and Rosie went with her. They didn't look very happy with Sparkleton, either.

Sparkleton felt bad. He hadn't meant to make anyone angry. But then he remembered that he wouldn't have to fail the test today, and he felt better. He trotted over to Willow and Gabe.

"Let me tell you about my new plan to get wish-granting magic," he said. He wanted to tell *the whole class* about his sparkletastic new plan. But all the rest of his friends were over on the other side of the meadow. Sparkleton wondered what they were talking about.

"That was a crummy thing to do, Sparkleton," Gabe said. "You should have just studied for the test."

"That's true," Willow chimed in. "On the other hand, did you see how bonkers that was? Utter mayhem! Pandemonium! Skunks everywhere!"

Willow and Sparkleton knocked hooves together in a unicorn high five.

"Sparkleton!" a voice cried. Sparkleton looked up and there was Rosie trotting toward them. She had a big, friendly smile on her face.

"I was just curious," she said to Sparkleton, "have you ever heard of the *Haunted Woods*?"

3

You're So Brave, Sparkleton!

"**N**ever heard of it," Sparkleton said.

"You *haven't?*" Rosie asked. "The Haunted Woods is a spooky, haunted forest. If you spend the *whole night* there . . ."

Rosie paused dramatically. Sparkleton's eyes were wide. What was she going to say?

Rosie took a deep breath, and then she whispered, "You wake up in the morning with *wish-granting magic!*"

Sparkleton's eyes got even wider.

"And nobody's ever done it before! It's just *too scary*!" Rosie said. "Sparkleton, you could be the *first one*!"

"The first one," Sparkleton said dreamily.

Rosie was getting more and more excited as she went on. "You should *definitely* go," she said. "I'm sure *you* can spend the whole night, Sparkleton. You're *so brave*! You probably won't even *notice* the hideous howling of the Whirlwind Unicorn."

Sparkleton shivered. That sounded pretty scary. "What's the Whirlwind Unicorn?" he asked.

"Oh, it's no big deal," Rosie said. "It's just the terrifying ghost that stalks the Haunted Woods. It only comes out at night. But don't worry, you'll hear it coming *long* before it arrives to drive you mad with fear."

Rosie lowered her voice. Sparkleton leaned in so he could hear what she was saying. "First," Rosie whispered, "you hear the thumping."

Sparkleton swallowed hard.

"Then," she went on, her voice even softer, "you hear the scratching."

Sparkleton's knees trembled a little.

"And finally," Rosie finished, her eyes as wide as saucers, "you hear its voice, howling in the wind as it moans your name. It knows your name, Sparkleton! And it's gonna get you!"

Whirlwind
Unicorn

Sparkleton's skin prickled all over. His mane stood on end.

"Wow," Gabe whispered. "That's pretty scary, Rosie."

"Yeah," Willow agreed. "It sounds awful. So, we're going tonight, right, Sparkleton?"

"Of *course* we are!" Sparkleton cried. "Whirlwind, schmirlwind. I'm not going to let a spooky ghost scare me away from *wish-granting magic*."

Rosie pranced enthusiastically. "Great!" she

said. "It isn't too far. First you have to cross the Glittering Stream. Then you pass through the Rocky Gorge. After that, you head straight to the Sparkling Boulder. And the Haunted Woods are right there! See?"

Rosie pushed a map toward Sparkleton and he bent down to look at it.

"Have fun, Sparkleton!" Rosie said. "Remember, you'll have to spend the *whole night* in order to get wish-granting magic—until sunrise! And don't worry, I'm sure the Whirlwind Unicorn won't trap you in a supernatural tornado or anything!" She trotted off, her tail swishing cheerfully behind her.

"This is going to be *sparkletastic*," Willow said.

"That's not the word I would have chosen," Gabe said.

But Sparkleton noticed

something: Gabe did *not* say "Count me out." He was coming with them. *Good old Gabe*, Sparkleton thought. He really was a loyal friend, even if he was a grouch.

The three friends spent the rest of the afternoon planning for their nighttime adventure. They studied Rosie's map. They gathered snacks. And they wondered a lot about the Whirlwind Unicorn.

"Maybe it's not a ghost," Willow said.

"Maybe it's an actual whirlwind," Gabe said. "Just some weird weather thing that happens in those woods sometimes."

"Maybe it's made up," Sparkleton said. "I bet it isn't even real."

But he kept hearing Rosie's voice in his head.

It knows your name, Sparkleton! And it's gonna get you!

4

We're Lost Already?

When it was bedtime, Sparkleton lay down in his soft bed of grass. He looked at the last purple streaks of sunset in the sky. Soon he heard his sister, Nella, and Gramma Una snoring softly. Time to go!

Sparkleton sprang up, grabbed the saddlebag he had stashed next to his bed, and trotted out of the little glen their family lived in.

Dear Gramma Una and Nella,
If you wake up and I am gone, it is
definitely not because I have run
away to the Haunted Woods.
    Love,
    SPARKLETON

Gabe and Willow joined him as he trotted away from Shimmer Lake. Gabe was carrying a basket full of glowing mushrooms.

"I grew these glow-in-the-dark mushrooms in my garden," Gabe said proudly. "They can light our way."

Sparkleton bumped shoulders with his friend in a unicorn hug.

"I brought stuff, too," Willow said. She was carrying two saddlebags across her back. "Things for our campsite, to make it cozy and nice!"

Sparkleton's friends were the best.

"You know where we're going, right, Sparkleton?" Gabe asked nervously as they trotted along.

Sparkleton nodded. "The Glittering Stream is on the other side of that hill," he said. He pointed with his nose at a big hill in the distance. The sky was getting darker by the minute, but you could still see the hill against the purple sky.

Sparkleton smiled. This was fun! Some blue flowers blooming at the edge of the path gave the night air a sweet smell. The stars twinkled peacefully in the sky. Sparkleton noticed a very big and bright star to the left. *That must be the Unicorn Star*, he thought.

"What did Rosie say about the Whirlwind Unicorn?" Gabe asked nervously as they made their way toward the hill.

Sparkleton looked around. Something was different . . . Then he realized. It had gotten so dark that he couldn't see the hill anymore. He was completely turned around.

"What direction is the hill?" Sparkleton asked his friends.

"Over there," Gabe said, pointing his horn to the right.

"No, over *there*," Willow said, pointing hers to the left.

None of them could see anything beyond the

soft glow of the mushrooms in Gabe's basket.

"We're lost *already*?" Gabe said. But Sparkleton was thinking hard. Something was tickling his memory . . . something about navigating at night.

That was it!

"I know *exactly* what direction we should be going in!" he cried. "When we were going toward the hill, the Unicorn Star was on our left! That means if we stand with the Unicorn Star on our left . . ."

"We'll be pointed at the hill!" Willow finished for him. "Brilliant, Sparkleton!"

The friends trotted on, keeping the Unicorn Star to their left. Soon they came to the hill. And on the other side was the Glittering Stream—just like on Rosie's map.

You've already read four chapters and 1,997 words! What a SHIMMERRIFIC effort!

5

He's a Good Friend

Sparkleton and his friends stood at the edge of the Glittering Stream. It was beautiful. It was also flowing fast.

Willow stuck a stick into the water. "It's not deep," she said. "But it's going to be hard to get across. The water is moving so rapidly."

Gabe dipped a hoof in. "Brr," he said. "And it's *cold*."

Sparkleton paced up and down the bank of the stream. He was thinking hard. "Maybe—" he started. But Gabe interrupted him.

"Did I mention the water is cold?" Gabe went on nervously. "And, oh my *stars*, it's late. I'm tired. Is anyone else tired? It's really dark, isn't it?"

Gabe was talking much faster than he usually did.

There's something he's not saying, Sparkleton thought. He'd known Gabe for a very long time. He could tell there was something wrong. And then, suddenly, he knew.

Gabe was scared.

Sparkleton nodded understandingly. "It's okay, Gabe," he said. "I get it." He stepped closer to his friend and bumped him gently with his nose. "You got us this far. Go home, and don't worry about it."

Gabe gave him a grateful look. He bumped Sparkleton back.

"Take these," Gabe said, setting down the basket of glowing mushrooms.

The three friends all tapped horns in farewell.

Then Gabe turned away. But just before he disappeared over the top of the hill, he turned back again.

"This will help light your way," he called. "And mine, too!" He used his confetti magic to send up a volley of fireworks. They rocketed high into the sky. Sparkleton grinned. He knew these fireworks. They lasted for *hours*.

Sparkleton picked up the basket of mushrooms. Then he and Willow turned back to face the stream.

"If we try to wade across it, it could sweep us right back to Shimmer Lake," Willow said. "We'd end up back home before we even got started!"

The two friends stared at the dark, shimmering water. It burbled as it ran—it almost sounded like it was laughing at them.

Sparkleton stamped a hoof. "I can't believe

we're already stuck," he said.

Willow shook her head. "We can't give up yet," she said. "You know my motto . . ."

"Never lick an angry worm?" he tried.

"That's a good one," Willow said. "But no."

"It's always goblin time somewhere?"

"Truer words were never spoken," Willow said. "But no."

"No idea," Willow said. "I just like how it sounds."

Sparkleton flattened his ears. Sometimes Willow was very unhelpful. But then—

"Wait," he said. "That gives me an idea!" He looked around. Aha!

"See that rock?" he said. He pointed a hoof at a rock sticking out of the stream. "And that one?" He pointed at another one. "We can hop

from rock to rock. And we won't even have to get our hooves wet!"

Willow gasped. "Sparkleton, you're a genius!" she said. "But if one of us slips . . ."

"We'll end up back at home, wet and cold," Sparkleton agreed. "And with no wish-granting magic."

"Then we better get this right," Willow said.

6

That Was Weird

Sparkleton took a deep breath and leapt.

His hooves hit the first stone with a *clack*. They hit the second stone with a *click*. And they hit the opposite bank with a *thonk*.

He was standing on the other side!

"Alley-oop!" Willow yelped, and hopped after him.

They'd done it!

According to Rosie's map, they had to cross a big meadow next. Then they'd be at the Rocky Gorge.

Sparkleton whistled a lively tune as they set out across the meadow. Crickets chirped cheerfully nearby, as though they were singing along.

Then the crickets stopped chirping.

There was a *snap* from a nearby bush. Sparkleton whirled around. But the bush was perfectly still.

Sparkleton and Willow looked at each other. "That was weird," Willow said. Her voice shook a little. Sparkleton swallowed hard. He was scared, too.

"What is *that*?" Willow cried a few minutes later. She was pointing her horn at a ghostly yellow light. It hovered in the air over the meadow and flickered in and out like a dying fire.

And then, as suddenly as it had appeared . . .

It was gone.

"Uh," Sparkleton said. He cleared his throat nervously. "Maybe it was the northern lights?"

"Sure," Willow said. She sounded spooked, too. "That must be it."

That was definitely not the northern lights, Sparkleton thought.

The two friends kept going, but the night didn't seem so friendly anymore. And the meadow was getting bumpier and rockier. It was hard to find footing in the dim moonlight.

"Ouch!" Willow cried. She stumbled sideways, almost falling. "My ankle!"

Sparkleton rushed to her side. She held up one of her hind hooves. "I twisted it," Willow said mournfully.

Sparkleton looked around. He spotted some tall, strong grass. He tore it up by the root and carefully wrapped it around Willow's ankle. A snug bandage would help support the joint.

"There," he said. He pulled it tight with his teeth. "Can you walk?"

Willow tested it out. She walked a few steps. "It feels stronger, Sparkleton, thank you!" she said. They kept going, but Sparkleton noticed that Willow was still limping.

Soon, Sparkleton and Willow reached the Rocky Gorge. It was a deep crack in the earth. It ran all the way across the meadow.

"The only way across is to jump," Willow said. She looked sad. "And I can't jump."

Sparkleton knew she was right.

"Don't worry about me," Willow said. "I'll wade into the Glittering Stream and it'll float me right back to Shimmer Lake. Gabe's fireworks will light my way home. I'm just sorry I won't get to see the Whirlwind Unicorn."

She put the saddlebags with the camping supplies over Sparkleton's back. "Goodbye, friend," she said. "Go get your wish-granting magic."

Sparkleton bumped noses with Willow. Then he walked up and down the side of the ravine a bit. He was testing the ground. Finally, he found the perfect spot to jump from. Not too muddy. Not too rocky. He backed up a few steps so he could get a running start.

Then Sparkleton lowered his head and launched himself into a gallop. Two strides, then three, then—

51

He was airborne!

Time seemed to slow down as Sparkleton leapt up over the deep ravine. From the air, he could see just how deep it was . . .

Suddenly, the other side looked very far away.

We made the leap! Only four more chapters until I get WISH-GRANTING MAGIC! Right?

7

TURN BACK BEFORE IT'S TOO LATE!

With a solid *thud*, Sparkleton landed safely on the other side of the Rocky Gorge.

He breathed out a deep sigh of relief. Then he reared up. He pawed at the air in a farewell salute to Willow.

"Good luck, Sparkleton!" she called. He watched wistfully as she limped back into the darkness. He knew she'd be fine. But would *he* be fine?

53

Sparkleton shivered. He double-checked that the Unicorn Star was still on his left, and set out to find the Sparkling Boulder. The Haunted Woods would be right after that.

Crrrk! Crrrk!

Sparkleton jumped. What was that weird scratching sound?

Probably just some harmless animal, he thought. But he trotted a little faster anyway.

Suddenly, an angry face appeared in the gloom.

"Gah!" Sparkleton cried. He reared back

away from it. But as the shadows shifted, he realized . . . it was just a lumpy rock. The light from his glowing mushrooms had given it a scary face.

Nothing to be scared of, Sparkleton thought. *Rosie's spooky stories must be getting to me.* He shook his head and glanced up at the Unicorn Star again. It felt like a friend, guiding his way.

He continued on the path. But he hadn't gotten very far when—

"What in all that shimmers?!" Sparkleton said out loud. The creepy rock with the angry face was back! But how was that possible? Had he gotten turned around? He looked up at the Unicorn Star. There it was, shining on his left. He'd been going straight the whole time. But then how could the rock be here again?

"I wish Gabe and Willow were here," Sparkleton said. But they weren't. All Sparkleton had was . . . Sparkleton.

But that wasn't nothing. "I'm glitterrific!" Sparkleton reminded himself. "And Rosie said I was *brave*. I just have to keep being brave until the morning . . . and then I'll finally have my wish-granting magic!"

He decided to sing to keep his spirits up.

I'm brave from my horn to my hooves
And nothing frightens me.
I'll sleep in the Haunted Woods
Until dawn brightens me!

Soon, Sparkleton spotted something glimmering up ahead. It was the Sparkling Boulder! Behind it, a dark forest rose up. The branches of the trees shivered in the breeze. They scraped together and made an eerie creaking noise.

Crrrk! Crrrrrrrrrk!

As Sparkleton got closer to the boulder, he saw that there were signs all over it.

WELCOME TO THE HAUNTED WOODS!

TURN BACK BEFORE IT'S TOO LATE!

Beware The Whirlwind Unicorn!

(ALSO NO LITTERING!)

Sparkleton shivered.

Maybe I should do like the sign says, he thought. *Maybe I should turn back now. Before it's too late.*

8

I'm Shimmerrific at Camping!

But Sparkleton did *not* turn and run. Instead, he took a deep breath. He gathered his courage and trotted boldly into the forest.

The trees in the Haunted Woods were mossy and dark. Their branches were twisted.

Something tugged Sparkleton's tail.

He whipped around, his heart pounding. But there was nobody there.

Maybe it was the wind, Sparkleton thought. He kept walking, deeper and deeper into the woods. Soon Sparkleton could hardly see the Unicorn Star.

"This is probably far enough," he said after a while. It was time to make camp.

Sparkleton didn't really know what would make a good camping spot. He'd never even *been* camping.

So he started thinking.

What if it rained?

Sparkleton decided to find a spot under some trees. "The leaves on the tree branches can keep me dry while I sleep," he said.

What if the ground was bumpy?

"Maybe I can find a spot with no stones," Sparkleton said. Or he could clear the stones away himself.

What if he got thirsty in the night?

"I bet there's a spring around here somewhere," Sparkleton said.

So he needed to find a flat spot, sheltered by trees, near some fresh water.

Sparkleton poked around the woods. He did his best to ignore the spooky noises and the creaking trees. Soon he smelled fresh water.

It was flat and sheltered, and there was a burbling little spring nearby. Sparkleton beamed. Finally, something had gone right!

Next, Sparkleton opened the saddlebag Willow had given him.

"Shimmerrific!" Sparkleton exclaimed. There was a nice dinner of alfalfa sprouts, a warm blanket, and a book.

Sparkleton smiled. Only Willow would want to read about goblins right before bed.

Sparkleton ate his dinner and settled inside

his tent for the night with Willow's blanket wrapped around him. He made a bed of leaves for extra warmth. "I'm *shimmerrific* at camping!" he said. Before he knew it, it would be morning . . . and he would finally have wish-granting magic. And with that thought in his mind, he closed his eyes.

Sparkleton was nearly asleep when he heard the sound.

Thud.

The thumping.

Thud. Thud. Thud.

Sparkleton's eyes widened.

First, you hear the thumping, Rosie had said. *Then you hear the scratching.* Was there going to be scratching next?!

Sparkleton's ears quivered, they were listening so hard.

Scrrrtch. Scrrrtch.

Sparkleton started to tremble.

And then the spooky voice, Rosie had said. Sparkleton burrowed further into his pile of leaves.

"*Ssssssssparkleton . . .*" an eerie voice whispered.

Sparkleton felt a shiver run down his back. It was happening just like Rosie said it would!

THUD.

THUD. THUD. THUD.

SCRRRTCH.   SCRRRTCH.

SSSSSSSSSPARKLETON...

And then he remembered the rest of what she'd said.

IT KNOWS YOUR NAME, SPARKLETON! AND IT'S GONNA GET YOU!

9

Ouch!

Sparkleton pulled the blanket over his head. Maybe if he hid *really well* . . .

"*Sssssssssparkleton* . . ." the voice hissed again. Sparkleton squeaked in fright. It was the Whirlwind Unicorn. It was nearby!

And then there was a *whoosh!* and a big wind swept away Sparkleton's blanket. His eyes popped open but he could hardly see a thing. Dirt swirled in the air around him.

It seemed like the Whirlwind Unicorn was . . . *everywhere*! First he heard it on his left, then on his right. Was he in the middle of it? Or was it just moving really fast? What was going on?

"SSSSSSSSSPARKLETON!!!"

Oh, that scary voice again! Sparkleton moved away from it until he backed into a tree trunk. He was trapped!

SSSSSSSSSPARKLETON!!!

I'm done for, Sparkleton thought. The wind whipped at his mane. *I'm never going home and everyone in Shimmer Lake will miss me forever.*

"SSSSSSSSSPAR—*yikes!*"

The Whirlwind Unicorn yelped in a pretty un-scary way. And the wind . . . stopped. Sparkleton blinked his eyes. He could see again!

"Ouch!" the Whirlwind Unicorn said. Except it wasn't the Whirlwind Unicorn. It was—

"Dale!" Sparkleton cried. He leapt up and galloped over to his friend. Dale was flopped over on the ground. His eyes were glassy and he looked kind of sick.

"I'm *so dizzy*," Dale moaned. He tried to stand up, but he fell over again right away.

"I don't understand," Sparkleton said. "Did the Whirlwind Unicorn get you? Where did it go?"

Dale looked embarrassed.

"*Wait a second*," Sparkleton said. Suddenly he understood perfectly. "*You* were the Whirlwind Unicorn. I mean, there *is* no Whirlwind Unicorn! You used your super speed to whirl around really fast! It was a trick!"

Dale hung his head. Sparkleton was feeling pretty annoyed. "Are these woods even haunted, or is that a trick, too?" he asked. Then something even worse occurred to him. "I'm not going to get wish-granting magic, am I?"

"That's right," someone said. "We made it all up." Sparkleton spun around, and there was Rosie—and Zuzu, and Britta, and Twinkle, and even his sister, Nella!

"You guys wanted to teach me a lesson for screwing up the wilderness survival test," Sparkleton said. He got it. He'd messed up everyone's day. Britta still smelled like skunk.

They'd all been mad at him—but he hadn't realized *how* mad.

"Well," Rosie said, "yeah, kind of. But not the way you think. Sure, we were mad at first—"

"I'm still mad," Britta said.

"But then we got to thinking," Twinkle said. "If you couldn't come with us on the camping trip, we'd really miss you!"

"I wouldn't," Britta said.

"So we decided to teach you a lesson . . ." Zuzu went on.

"A *camping* lesson!" Dale explained.

Sparkleton's eyes widened. The Unicorn Star . . . crossing the stream . . . jumping the gorge . . . finding the perfect camping spot . . .

YOU TRICKED ME INTO **STUDYING!**

"That's right!" Twinkle said. "We wanted to help you!"

"I didn't," Britta said.

"Well," Rosie said, "the rest of us did. And it worked! You'll pass the test now for sure, Sparkleton!"

Only 557 words left to read and I still smell like a SKUNK!

10

Good Work, Sparkleton!

"I studied for the test all over again!" Rosie bragged.

"I made even more flash cards!" Britta said.

"I read the book *six more times*," Dale announced.

Sparkleton grinned happily. It was two days later and the young unicorns of Shimmer Lake were gathered in Gramma Una's classroom. All the books were back in place, and it hardly smelled at all. They were finally going to take the wilderness survival test. And this time, Sparkleton was looking forward to it.

"Settle in, younglings!" Gramma Una said. She trotted up to the front of the classroom glen. Sparkleton winced when he got to his spot. He was sitting next to Britta, and she still smelled pretty bad.

Gramma Una passed out the exams, and Sparkleton got to work.

NAME: SPARKLETON

Which star can you use to navigate at night?

The Unicorn Star

Clever me →

How can you cross a river that's flowing very fast?

Hop on rocks

What do you need to watch out for when you're jumping over a gorge? Jump from solid ground.

Not rocky! Not gravelly! Not muddy!!

#1 JUMPER!

What is the perfect camping spot?

Tree for shelter

 No rocks!

Fresh water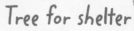

How can you stay warm at night when camping?

Pile of leaves
Bring a blanket!

BONUS: What can you do if you twist a hoof in the field?

Ouch!   Wrap with grass

Much better!

Gramma Una graded the exams quickly when the unicorns were done. All the young unicorns crowded around her.

"Everyone passes!" she said. "And everyone gets to go on the camping trip!"

HOORAY!

"Good work, Sparkleton!" Willow said. She trotted over to him with a springy step. The healing unicorns had fixed her ankle.

"Yeah," Gabe said. "I guess you ended up learning about camping after all."

"I sure did!" Sparkleton said proudly. "And I learned something else while I was out there, too."

"The meaning of responsibility?" Gabe asked hopefully.

"The secret of the goblin king?" Willow asked eagerly.

"No," Sparkleton said. "I learned how to make someone's day better. Here, watch this."

He pulled a beautiful wreath made of blue flowers out from under the bush where he had hidden it.

"Britta!" he called.

Britta walked over with a sour look on her face. "What?" she said. Sparkleton worked hard not to wrinkle his nose.

"Here," he said. He offered her the wreath of sweet-smelling blue flowers. "I made this for you."

Britta poked her head through the wreath. Suddenly, the skunk smell vanished.

"I don't stink anymore!" Britta said. She pranced in place. "Thank you, Sparkleton!"

"So do you forgive me for getting you sprayed in the face by a skunk so I could skip a test I should have just studied for?" Sparkleton asked.

"Absolutely not!" Britta said cheerfully. "We're enemies for life now!"

She trotted away to show off the wreath to the other unicorns.

"But thanks for the wreath," Britta said.

Sparkleton had never had an enemy for life. He thought it sounded kind of neat.

"So anyway," Sparkleton told Willow and Gabe. "I've been thinking."

"Always a dangerous idea, but go on," Willow said.

"I've been thinking," Sparkleton continued. "I didn't get my wish-granting magic. Yet. But I did have a really cool adventure with you guys. And you know what's even more magical than granting wishes?"

Goblins?

CONGRATULATIONS!

You've read **10** chapters,

87 pages,

and **5,324** words!

What a **WHIRLWIND**! How do you feel?

All your **SPARKLETASTIC EFFORT** paid off!

What will you read **NEXT**?

There's a great book about the **GOBLIN KING**.

UNICORN GAMES

THINK!

Sparkleton, Willow, and Gabe are BFFs. Make a list of all the words that describe a good friend. Then circle the three traits that are most important to you!

FEEL!

In this book, Sparkleton tries to spend a night in the Haunted Woods—even though he is scared. Write about a time you were afraid to do something but tried it anyway. How did you feel?

ACT!

Draw a picture of yourself camping in the woods with your friends. What would you bring with you? What fun things would you do together? What would you do if you saw the Whirlwind Unicorn?

Illustrated by Hollie Mengert

CALLIOPE GLASS is a writer and editor. She lives in New York City with two small humans and one big human, and a hardworking family of house spiders who are all named Gwen. There are no unicorns in her apartment, but they are always welcome.

Photo by Mike McCain

HOLLIE MENGERT is an illustrator and animator living in Los Angeles. She loves drawing animals, making people smile with her work, and spending time with her amazingly supportive family and friends.